What's happening on the farm?

Heather Amery
Illustrated by Stephen Cartwright

Consultant: Betty Root

A visit to the hens

Can you see how many eggs the hens have laid?
Who is asleep in the hen house?

Can you name all the animals in the picture?
What is the horse doing?

Shearing the sheep

Sheep need to have their woolly coats cut off in summertime.
Can you see which sheep is being sheared at the moment?

Which animal shouldn't be in the sheep pen?
One lamb is missing from the pens. Can you find it?

Looking at the pigs

How many pigs can you see?
How many are piglets?

Pigs eat from a trough.
Which other animal is looking for food?

Feeding the ducks

Baby ducks are ducklings and baby geese are goslings.
How many of each can you see?

Which duckling is getting a ride?
What other animals can you see around the pond?

Milking time for the cows

Cows need to be milked every day.
Which cow doesn't want to be milked?

Who is going to get wet?
Who is slipping in the mud?

Picking the apples

How many different animals can you see?
How many apple trees are there?

Who is picking apples?
Who is eating them?

By the barn

How many kittens are there?
Find 2 white hens and 3 mice.

What has happened to the trailer?
Who has lost a shoe?

Match the mothers with their babies

What are the baby animals called?

First published in 1984 by Usborne Publishing Ltd., Usborne House, 83-85 Saffron Hill, London EC1N 8RT, England. www.usborne.com
Copyright © 2005, 1992, 1984 Usborne Publishing Ltd. First Published in America 1993. This edition Published in America in 2006.